This book belongs to:

_____

Contents

Cover illustration by Julian Mosedale

Published by Ladybird Books Ltd
80 Strand London WC2R ORL
A Penguin Company

8 10 9

© LADYBIRD BOOKS LTD MCMXCVII, MMI

LADYBIRD and the device of a Ladybird are trademarks of Ladybird Books Ltd

Printed in China

My dad can't dance

written by Lorraine Horsley
illustrated by Julian Mosedale

My dad can't dance,

and my mum can't sing.

My brother can't paint,

and I can't do a thing.

My sister can't skip,

and the baby can't talk.

Our cat can't climb,

and our dog won't walk.

Grandad can't cook,

and Granny can't knit.

Their cat can't climb,

and their dog won't sit.

When you look at us,
it's plain to see,

we can't do much,
but we're a great family.

When I broke my leg

written by Catriona Macgregor

illustrated by Harmen van Straaten

When I broke my leg,
Lucy came round with
her friend from school.

13

When I broke my leg,
Sam came round
to watch TV.

14

When I broke my leg,
Ben came round with
lots of comics.

When I broke my leg,
Gran came round with
a great big cake.

It was **great**, when I broke my leg!

My diary

written by Shirley Jackson

illustrated by Dave McTaggart

We went to our new house
in a new town.
I don't like it here.

Monday

I went to my new school.
I was on my own.

Tuesday

I made my first friend.
He is called James.

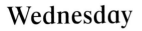

Wednesday

I helped my teacher
to put up my painting.
James put his up too.

Thursday

I made lots more friends.
I'm not on my own now.

Friday

Our class went swimming
in the big pool.
I was the best swimmer.

Saturday

It was James's birthday.
I went to his party.
All our friends came too.
I really like my new town.

A rough ride home

written by Shirley Jackson
illustrated by Ant Parker

The car went up the hill,

over the hill,

down the hill fast.

Round the bend,

down the bend,

along the road at last.

29

The drinks were too fizzy.

The rides made me dizzy.

The car made me sick.

"Let me out. Quick!"

A rough ride home

Encourage your child to
read this several times so that
he memorises the rhyme and enjoys reading it with
increasing fluency. Help him to notice the spelling
patterns in the rhyming words:

f ast
l ast

f izzy
d izzy

Have fun making other words using these
endings, such as 'blast', or building
nonsense words like 'zizzy'.

New words

Encourage your child to use some of
these new words in this list to make
up his own stories and rhymes.
Go back to look at earlier books
and their wordlists to practise
other words.

Read with Ladybird

Read with Ladybird has been written to help you to help your child:

- to take the first steps in reading
- to improve early reading progress
- to gain confidence

Main Features

- **Several stories and rhymes in each book**

This means that there is not too much for you and your child to read in one go.

- **Rhyme and rhythm**

Read with Ladybird uses rhymes or stories with a rhythm to help your child to predict and memorise new words.

- **Gradual introduction and repetition of key words**

Read with Ladybird introduces and repeats the 100 most frequently used words in the English language.

- **Compatible with school reading schemes**

The key words that your child will learn are compatible with the word lists that are used in schools. This means that you can be confident that practising at home will support work done at school.

- **Information pullout**

Use this pullout to understand more about how you can use each story to help your child to learn to read.

But the most important feature of **Read with Ladybird** is for you and your child to have fun sharing the stories and rhymes with each other.